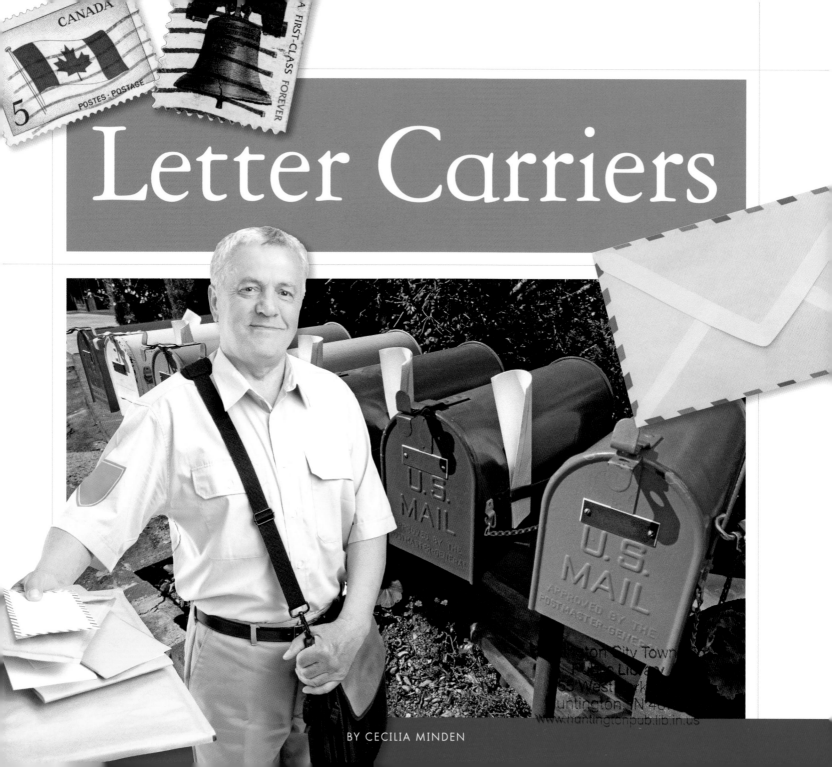

Letter Carriers

BY CECILIA MINDEN

The Child's World®

Published by The Child's World®
1980 Lookout Drive • Mankato, MN 56003-1705
800-599-READ • www.childsworld.com

Acknowledgments
The Child's World®: Mary Berendes, Publishing Director
The Design Lab: Design
Jody Jensen Shaffer: Editing
Pamela J. Mitsakos: Photo Research

Photos
BassittART/iStock.com: 6-7, 12; belterz/iStock.com:
Canadian stamp; Captainflash/iStock.com: 8; Claudia
Walpole: 9, 14; dardespot/iStock.com: 16; GlobalP/
iStock.com: 19; hartcreations/iStock.com: 4; Hemera/
Thinkstock.com: 5; Juanmonino /iStock.com: 20-21;
Kathleen Petelinsek: 22; Ljupco/iStock.com: cover, 1;
LuckyBusiness/iStock.com: 10-11; PhotoDisc: mailbox,
mailbox row, Photographerlondon/Dreamstime.com:
18; Skystorm/iStock.com: envelope; traveler1116/
iStock.com: liberty stamp; uniball/iStock.com:
USMailbox

ISBN 9781626870147
LCCN 2013947293

Printed in the United States of America
Mankato, MN
December, 2013
PA02191

ABOUT THE AUTHOR

Dr. Cecilia Minden is a university professor and reading specialist with classroom and administrative experience in grades K–12. She earned her PhD in reading education from the University of Virginia.

CONTENTS

Hello, My Name Is Max.

Hello. My name is Max. Many people live and work in my neighborhood. Each of them helps the neighborhood in different ways.

I thought of all the things I like to do. I like to be outside. I like to take long walks in my neighborhood. I have a good memory for names and faces. How could I help my neighborhood when I grow up?

I Could Be a Letter Carrier!

Letter carriers get to be outside much of the day. They know everybody in the neighborhood.

Best of all, letter carriers make people happy when they deliver cards and letters from family and friends.

Letter carriers get to know the neighborhood by delivering the mail.

Learn About This Neighborhood Helper!

The best way to learn is to ask questions. Words such as *who*, *what*, *where*, *when*, and *why* will help me learn about being a letter carrier.

Where Can I Learn More?
National Association of Letter Carriers
100 Indiana Avenue NW
Washington, DC 20001-2144

U.S. Postal Service Headquarters
Personnel Division
475 L'Enfant Plaza SW, Room 1813
Washington, DC 20260-4261

Asking a letter carrier questions will help you learn more about the job.

Who Can Become a Letter Carrier?

Boys and girls who have good memories may want to become letter carriers. Letter carriers also need to be friendly and enjoy working with the public.

Letter carriers are important neighborhood helpers. They bring cards, letters, packages, and magazines to people's front doors.

**How Can I Explore
This Job?**
Talk to your local letter carrier
when she comes to your
home. How long has she
worked for the Postal Service?
What is a typical workday
like for her? What does she
like best about her job?

Letter carriers must always be friendly when dealing with the public.

Meet a Letter Carrier!

This is Peter Walpole. Peter has been a letter carrier for eighteen years. He works in Charlottesville, Virginia. When Peter is not delivering the mail, he likes to spend time with his family, write stories, and play golf.

How Many Letter Carriers Are There?
About 334,000 people work as letter carriers.

Peter has worked as a letter carrier since 1987.

Where Can I Learn to Be a Letter Carrier?

People who want to be letter carriers need to get a high score on a special test given by the United States Postal Service. Having a good memory will help you get a high score!

Letter carriers must first pass a special test.

New letter carriers get training from other workers before they start delivering the mail. They learn how to organize the mail and where to deliver it.

How Much School Will I Need?

Letter carriers must have a high school diploma. They also must pass a written test and take a physical exam.

Letter carriers deliver mail by walking and driving through neighborhoods.

What Does a Letter Carrier Need to Do the Job?

Peter drives a postal truck made just for delivering mail. Inside his truck are places to put bundles of letters and **parcels**.

The first thing Peter does when he goes to work is check his truck to make sure the lights and engine are working. He won't be able to deliver the mail if his truck doesn't work!

What Are Some Tools I Will Use?
- Mail bag
- Mail cart
- Mail truck

What Clothes Will I Wear?

- Comfortable walking shoes
- Postal uniform

Peter also has to know special words that letter carriers use to describe their work. For example, Peter uses big rubber bands to hold the letters together. This is called "strapping out" the mail. Knowing these special words makes it easier for Peter to communicate with other letter carriers.

Peter follows a mail route when he works.

Where Does a Letter Carrier Work?

Peter works at a post office. He goes to work early in the morning when most people are still asleep. He then begins sorting mail into the proper delivery order for his **route**. Next he loads the mail and packages for that day into his truck.

Peter delivers the mail to each stop along his route until lunchtime. Then he takes a break for about half an hour. Peter delivers the mail along the rest of his route after lunch. He also picks up mail that has been dropped in mailboxes.

What's It Like Where I'll Work?
Some letter carriers walk to deliver the mail. These carriers are outside in all sorts of weather—sometimes very hot, sometimes very cold. Other letter carriers drive a car or truck.

Peter delivers the mail to his last stop and then drives back to the post office. He puts the mail he has picked up in a big hamper for **postal clerks** to sort.

Clerks and mail handlers help sort the mail for letter carriers.

Who Works with Letter Carriers?

The U.S. Postal Service is a very large operation. Clerks and mail handlers bring Peter the mail for his route each day. There are also truck drivers, airplane pilots, and special police officers called postal inspectors. Maintenance crews care for the postal trucks, buildings, and equipment and make sure everything is working properly. These people work together every day to make sure the mail gets delivered.

What other Jobs Might I Like?
- Courier and messenger
- Meter reader
- Postal clerk
- Subway operator

Some letter carriers are also responsible for picking up mail that people drop in mailboxes.

Letter carriers sometimes face unfriendly animals along their route.

When Does a Letter Carrier Have to Be Extra Careful?

Did you know Dog Bite Prevention Week is in May? The U.S. Postal Service reports more than 3,000 dog bites each year. Most dogs on a letter carrier's route are friendly, but workers need to know how to avoid animals that are not friendly.

How Might My Job Change?
Letter carriers get more experience and eventually get better routes. Some letter carriers move into jobs where they are in charge of other letter carriers.

I Want to Be a Letter Carrier!

I think being a letter carrier would be a great way to be a neighborhood helper. Someday I may be the person you see delivering mail in your neighborhood!

Is This Job Growing?
The need for letter carriers will not grow.

Why Don't You Try Being a Letter Carrier?

Do you think you would like to be a letter carrier? You need to know how to check an envelope to make sure it includes all the right information.

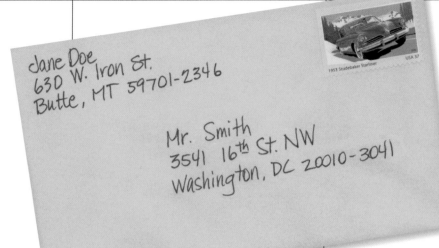

Jane Doe
630 W. Iron St.
Butte, MT 59701-2346

1953 Studebaker Starliner   USA 37

Mr. Smith
3541 16th St. NW
Washington, DC 20010-3041

Look at this envelope and answer these questions:

- Is the writing easy to read?
- Does the address include the name and street address?
- Does the address include the city, state, and zip code?
- Is there a return address in the upper left-hand corner?
- Is there enough postage?
- Do you think a letter carrier would deliver this letter?

GLOSSARY

parcels (PAR-sulz) packages

postal clerks (POST-ul KLURKS) postal workers who sort through and organize mail

route (ROWT) a path or course that is mapped out

LEARN MORE ABOUT LETTER CARRIERS

BOOKS

Flanagan, Alice. *Here Comes Mr. Eventoff with the Mail!* Danbury, CT: Children's Press, 1998.

Knudsen, Shannon. *Postal Workers.* Minneapolis, MN: Lerner Publications, 2006.

Kottke, Jan. *A Day with a Mail Carrier.* Danbury, CT: Children's Press, 2000.

WEB SITES

Visit our home page for lots of links about letter carriers:

www.childsworld.com/links

Note to Parents, Teachers, and Librarians: We routinely check our Web links to make sure they're safe, active sites—so encourage your readers to check them out!

INDEX